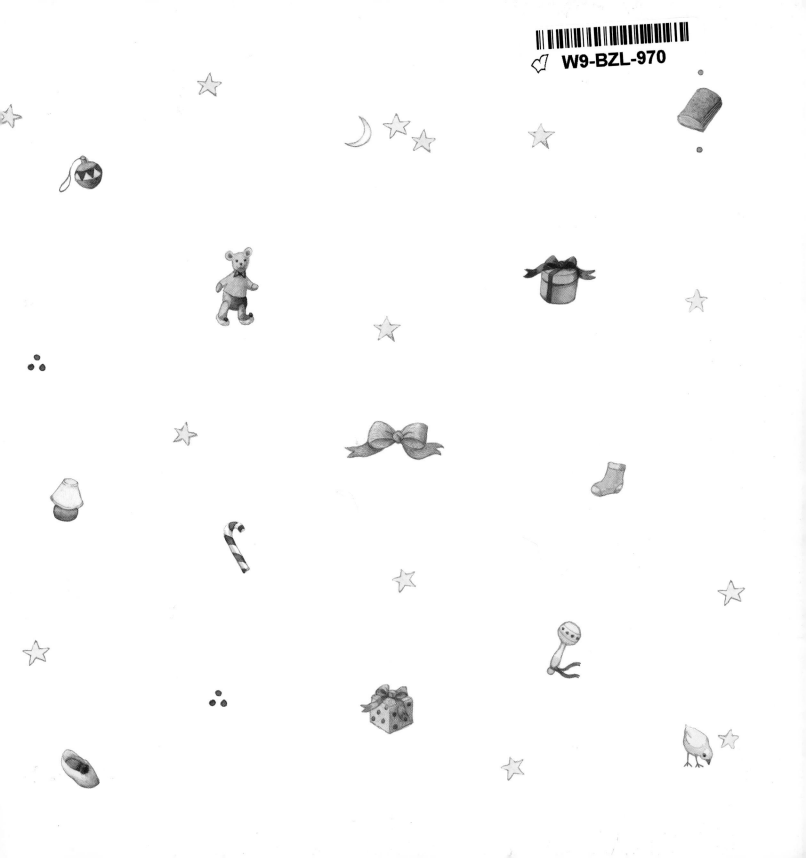

For Freya
—M.K.

Daddy's Little Girl
Words and music copyright © 1949, 1977 by Cherio Corp.
Illustrations copyright © 2004 by Maggie Kneen
Manufactured in China by South China Printing Company Ltd.

www.harperchildrens.com

Library of Congress Cataloging-in-Publication Data
Burke, Bobby.
    Daddy's little girl / words and music by Bobby Burke and
Horace Gerlach ; pictures by Maggie Kneen.—1st ed.
        p.   cm.
    Summary: An illustrated version of a song which describes
how special a daughter is to her father.
    ISBN 0-06-028722-5
    [1. Children's songs, English—Texts. 2. Fathers and daughters—
Songs and music. 3. Songs.] I. Gerlach, Horace. II. Kneen,
Maggie, ill. III. Title.
PZ8.3.B95248Dad 2004
782.42164'0268—dc21
                                                        2003008336

Typography by Jeanne L. Hogle
1 2 3 4 5 6 7 8 9 10
❖
First Edition

Daddy's Little Girl

Words and music by Bobby Burke and Horace Gerlach
Pictures by Maggie Kneen

HarperCollinsPublishers

Y ou're the end of the rainbow, my pot of gold,

You're Daddy's little girl to have and hold;

A precious gem is what you are,

You're Mommy's bright and shining star;

You're the spirit of Christmas, my star on the tree,

You're the Easter bunny to Mommy and me;

You're sugar, you're spice, you're everything nice,
And you're Daddy's little girl.

You're the end of the rainbow, my pot of gold,
You're Daddy's little girl to have and hold;

A precious gem is what you are,
You're Mommy's bright and shining star;

You're the treasure I cherish, so sparkling and bright,
You were touched by holy and beautiful light;

Like angels that sing, a heavenly thing,
And you're Daddy's little girl.

DADDY'S LITTLE GIRL

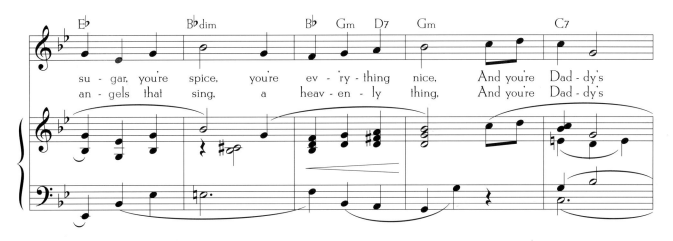